DATE DUE

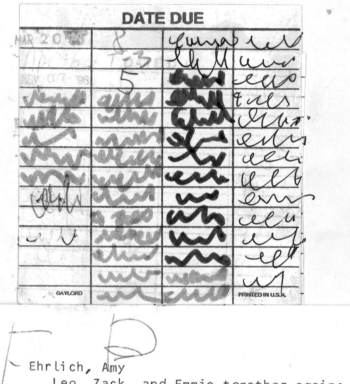

MAR 20	8		
	T-53		
NOV 07 96	5		

GAYLORD   PRINTED IN U.S.A.

E
E
c.1

Ehrlich, Amy
    Leo, Zack, and Emmie together again;
pictures by Steven Kellogg.   New York, Dial
Bks. for Young Readers, 1987.
    56 p. ill. col. draws.

1. Friendship-Fict. 2. Short stories
I. Title

LEO, ZACK, AND EMMIE TOGETHER AGAIN

* by Amy Ehrlich *
pictures by Steven Kellogg

DIAL BOOKS FOR YOUNG READERS • New York

Dial easy-to-read

For the real
ZACK AND EMMIE
Love A.E.

For PHYLLIS
AND ATHA AND AMY
AND DAVID AND SHELLY
AND REGINA
AND DOROTHY AND BARBARA AND Everyone Else in the Class

Love S.K.

Published by Dial Books for Young Readers
2 Park Avenue, New York, New York 10016

Published simultaneously in Canada by
Fitzhenry & Whiteside Limited, Toronto
Text copyright © 1987 by Amy Ehrlich
Pictures copyright © 1987 by Steven Kellogg
All rights reserved
Printed in Hong Kong by South China Printing Co.
The Dial Easy-to-Read logo is a trademark of
Dial Books for Young Readers,
a division of NAL Penguin Inc., ® TM 1,162,718.
COBE
2 4 6 8 10 9 7 5 3
Library of Congress Cataloging-in-Publication Data
Ehrlich, Amy, 1942– Leo, Zack, and Emmie together again.
Summary: A trio of friends spends the winter of their second grade
making snowballs and Valentine cards, going to a Christmas party,
and fighting a bout with chicken pox.
[1. Friendship—Fiction.] I. Kellogg, Steven, ill.
II. Title. III. Series.
PZ7.E328Lf 1987   [E]   86-16810
ISBN 0-8037-0381-3
ISBN 0-8037-0382-1 (lib. bdg.)

Reading Level 2.2

CONTENTS

A SNOWY DAY

Leo, Zack, and Emmie

were best friends.

Leo was the slowest runner.

Zack was the fastest.

But Emmie was very fast too.

One snowy day Zack raced outside.

"Yippee!" he shouted. "No school!"

He ran over to Leo's house.

Emmie was there already.

"Let's have a snowball fight,"

said Zack.

He threw a snowball at Emmie

but she ducked.

Instead it hit Leo

who was coming out the door.

"Okay for you, Zack!" Leo yelled.

But all the snowballs

Leo threw at Zack

missed him completely.

Only Zack could hit anyone.

"This is dumb," said Leo.

He walked away

rolling a snowball along the ground.

Emmie said to Zack,

"What do you want to do now?"

"How about a sled race?" said Zack.

"We'll get snow in our boots,"
said Emmie.

"We could build a fort," said Zack.

"It takes too long," said Emmie.

"We could bury each other
in the snow," said Zack.
"Too wet," said Emmie.

"Face it, Zack," she said,
"we're not having any fun."
"You're right," Zack said.
"Let's go find Leo."

Zack and Emmie followed the trail
Leo's snowball had made in the snow.
It led around a corner
and across a field.

Finally they saw Leo.
He was pushing a snowball
bigger than himself.

Four more giant snowballs
were lined up nearby.
And there was a pile
of smaller snowballs too.
"They're for snow people," said Leo.
"I want to make lots of them."

"Can we help?" asked Emmie.

"Sure," said Leo.

"But don't throw any snowballs at me."

They worked until the sun went down

and lights came on in the houses.

12

When they were through
they had a whole snow family.
A snow mother and father.
Snow sisters and brothers.
Even a snow baby.

The snow people were wearing
their hats and scarves and mittens.
Their jackets were wet
and their boots were full of snow.
But Leo, Zack, and Emmie
did not mind at all.

THE CHRISTMAS PARTY

Every year the second grade

had a big Christmas party.

"It's to be this Friday, class,"

said Miss Davis.

"We'll have a tree and a grab bag.

And if we're lucky, Santa will come."

Emmie passed Zack a note.

When he unfolded it,

the note said, "Fat chance."

"What did you mean, fat chance?"

Zack asked Emmie after school.

"There's no such thing

as Santa Claus," said Emmie.

"Everybody knows that."

"They do not!" Zack shouted.

He ran to Leo's house.

Leo was outside

stringing lights on pine trees

and listening to Christmas carols.

Leo loved Christmas.

Zack was sure Leo would tell him

that Santa Claus was real.

"Is there such a thing
as Santa Claus?" Zack asked.
Leo took off his baseball cap
and scratched his head.
"I'm not sure," he said at last.
"Why don't you ask Emmie?"

Zack gave up and walked away.

At the Christmas party

he'd find out for himself

if Santa Claus was real.

In the meantime he bought
jumping beans for the grab bag
and baked Christmas cookies
with red and green sprinkles.
Emmie came over
the day Zack baked cookies.

But he didn't want her to say

anything about Santa Claus,

so he pretended he wasn't home.

Finally it was time for the party.

Zack's cookies were a hit

and he got a new boomerang

in the grab bag.

But Zack didn't care.

He was waiting for Santa Claus.

Suddenly Miss Davis turned on

the Christmas tree lights

and put music on the record player.

The classroom door opened.

There stood a man in a red suit

with a long white beard.

He looked just like Santa Claus.

Everyone lined up
to sit on Santa's lap.
Emmie was first in line
and Leo was second.
Zack could not believe it!

Both of them hugged Santa
and said what they wanted
for Christmas.
But when Zack's turn came
he didn't ask for any presents.

Instead he stood on tiptoe

right next to Santa

and pulled his beard.

"You're real, aren't you?" Zack asked.

"Ouch, that hurt," said Santa Claus.

"Of course I'm real."

"I knew it all along," said Zack.

CHICKEN POX

Chicken pox was going around.

Everybody had it.

Finally Leo, Zack, Emmie,

and two other people

were the only ones left

in Miss Davis's class.

All the others were out sick.

"We're powerful," said Zack.
"That chicken pox won't mess
with us."

But the next day
Zack wasn't in school.
Leo and Emmie went to his house
to find out why.

Zack opened the door a crack.

He was in his pajamas

and his face was covered with spots.

"Don't come too close," said Zack.

"My mother says I'm catching."

Leo and Emmie moved back fast.

"I feel strange myself," Leo said.

"I think I might be getting it."

"That means I'm next," said Emmie.

But Emmie did not catch chicken pox.
For two days she and Linda Jones
were all alone in second grade.
Even though Miss Davis let them
read and draw pictures,
it wasn't really fun.

Finally people began getting over chicken pox.

The next week even Zack and Leo were back in school.

All anyone talked about
was chicken pox.
Mike said he'd had
spots on his tongue.

Polly said she'd had them

on the bottoms of her feet.

Steve said his mother had let him

drink all the ginger ale he wanted.

Rob said his father had played
Monopoly with him every day.

"Poor Emmie," said Zack at playtime.
"The chicken pox was great.
You really missed out."

Emmie walked away from him
and sat down on a bench.
She was so sick of hearing
about chicken pox
that her head hurt and she felt dizzy.

Hey, maybe this was it!

Maybe she had chicken pox at last!

That night Emmie's mother
gave her ginger ale in bed.

But Emmie was too sick to drink it.

The night after that, her father said
they could play Monopoly.
But Emmie was too sick
to set up the Monopoly board.

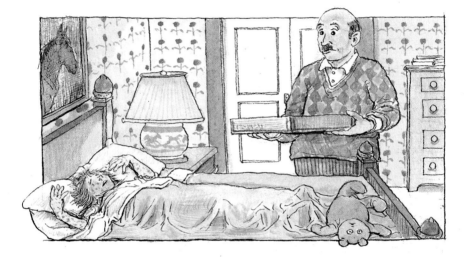

She had chicken pox on her knees,
her elbows, and everywhere else.
It itched like crazy
and she wasn't allowed to scratch.

One day when Emmie was feeling better,
Leo and Zack showed up.
They gave her a get-well card
and sat right down on her bed.

"You better be careful," said Emmie.

"I might still be catching."

Zack said, "I wouldn't mind getting

chicken pox again."

"Don't listen to him," said Leo.
"There's only one good thing
about chicken pox
and Zack knows it."
"What's that?" asked Emmie.
Leo gave her a big smile.
"You can only have it once,"
he said.

BE MY VALENTINE

Leo, Zack, and Emmie were
shopping in the five-and-ten.
They went up one row
and down another
until they came to a row
of valentine cards.

"Oh, goody!" said Emmie.
"Valentine's Day is my
favorite holiday."
"I think it stinks," said Zack.
"Only girls like Valentine's Day."

"I'm a boy and I like it," said Leo.
"You would," said Zack.

They got to the checkout line.

Emmie had picked out

pink hearts, red lace paper,

and gold and silver markers.

"Come over to my house," she said.

"We'll make our own valentine cards."

"Not me," said Zack. "Forget it."

He turned right

and Leo and Emmie turned left.

At Emmie's house

they spread everything out

on the kitchen table.

Then they drew and cut and pasted

all afternoon.

"I'm making cards

for the girls in our class

but not for the boys," said Emmie.

"I'm making cards for everyone,"
said Leo.

His cards were messier than Emmie's
but they were bigger too.

Leo was very proud of them.

On Valentine's Day

he got to school early

and sneaked into Miss Davis's class.

It was so early that it was still dark.

Leo left a valentine card

on each person's desk.

Then he went home for breakfast.

In the playground
before school started,
everyone was telling secrets
about Valentine's Day.
Some of the girls
kept pointing at Zack
and giggling.

"What's so funny?" Zack asked.

But they just giggled more

and ran away.

"I don't get it," said Zack.

"Those girls like you," said Emmie.

"You'll see."

Sure enough,

when they got to Miss Davis's room,

Zack's desk was piled high

with valentine cards.

Everyone else had at least one card
because Leo had made a card
for everyone.
But Leo didn't have any.

He tried not to feel bad.

It had been fun making the cards.

That's why he had done it.

After school Zack and Emmie
caught up with Leo.

"I'm sorry I didn't give you a card,"
said Emmie.

"All the ones I got were dumb,"
said Zack. "Yours was the best."

Leo stopped walking.

"You two are my friends, right?"
he asked.

"Right!" said Zack and Emmie.

"Okay," said Leo.

"Then I have one more question.

Will you be my valentine?"

"Sure!" Emmie said, giving him a hug.

"Valentine's Day is for girls,"
said Zack.

"Here we go again!" said Emmie.